Is that what friends do?

MARJORIE NEWMAN
ILLUSTRATED BY PETER BOWMAN

HUTCHINSON

London Sydney Auckland Johannesburg

Elephant sat gloomily on the river bank.

Monkey came dancing along.

'Hello, Elephant!' cried Monkey. 'All alone?'

'Yes,' sighed Elephant.

Is that what friends do?

To Amber - M.N.
To Nicola, my best friend - P.B.

First published in 1998

1 3 5 7 9 10 8 6 4 2

First published in the United Kingdom in 1998 by
Hutchinson Children's Books
Random House UK Limited
20 Vauxhall Bridge Road, London SW1V 2SA

Random House Australia (Pty) Limited
20 Alfred Street, Milsons Point, Sydney
New South Wales 2061, Australia

Random House New Zealand Limited
18 Poland Road, Glenfield
Auckland 10, New Zealand

Random House South Africa (Pty) Limited
Endulini, 5A Jubilee Road, Parktown 2193, South Africa

Random House UK Limited Reg. No. 954009

A CIP catalogue record for this book is available from the British Library

ISBN: 0 09 176609 5

Printed in Singapore

‘So am I!’ said Monkey. ‘Let’s be friends!’

'I've never had a friend before,' said Elephant.

'I have. Lots!' cried Monkey. 'Why don't you come and stay with me?'

'Is that what friends do?'
asked Elephant.

'Of course!' cried Monkey.

Monkey's doorway was too small for Elephant.

'Ow!' cried Elephant.

'Eee!' cried Elephant.

'Ah!' cried Elephant.
'I nearly got stuck.'

‘You are funny,’ cried Monkey, doubling up laughing, and not trying to help Elephant, *at all*.

Monkey switched on the radio. The music was very loud.

'Let's dance!' cried Monkey.

'Is that what friends do?' asked Elephant.

'Of course!' cried Monkey. 'Come on.'

'Ow!' cried Elephant.

'Eee!' cried Elephant.

'Ah!' cried Elephant.
'I can't dance.'

'You are funny,' cried Monkey, spinning round on one leg, and not trying to help Elephant, *at all*.

‘We’ll have scrambled eggs on toast for supper,’ said Monkey.

‘I don’t like scrambled eggs on toast,’ said Elephant.

‘I do!’ cried Monkey. ‘I’ll let you be cook and we’ll eat supper together.’

‘Is that what friends do?’ asked Elephant.

‘Of course!’ cried Monkey.

'Ah!' cried Elephant.

'Eee!' cried Elephant.

'Ow!' cried Elephant.
'I can't cook.'

'You are funny!' laughed Monkey, sitting up at the table, and not trying to help Elephant, *at all*.

'Bedtime,' announced Monkey. 'Stay the night and you can sleep in my chair.'

'Is that what friends do?' asked Elephant, trying to make himself comfortable.

'Of course,' yawned Monkey.

'Ow!' cried Elephant.

'Eee!' cried Elephant.

'Ah!' cried Elephant. 'I'm falling off.'

Monkey didn't even stir.
He slept very well. He
snored very loudly.

Elephant didn't sleep one wink. Not even with cotton wool stuffed into his ears.

Next morning, Monkey woke up early.

'Come on, Elephant,' he cried. 'Let's go climbing.'

'I don't like climbing, especially before breakfast,' said Elephant.

'I do,' cried Monkey. 'We can climb together.'

'Is that what friends do?' asked Elephant.

'Of course!' cried Monkey, putting on his jacket.

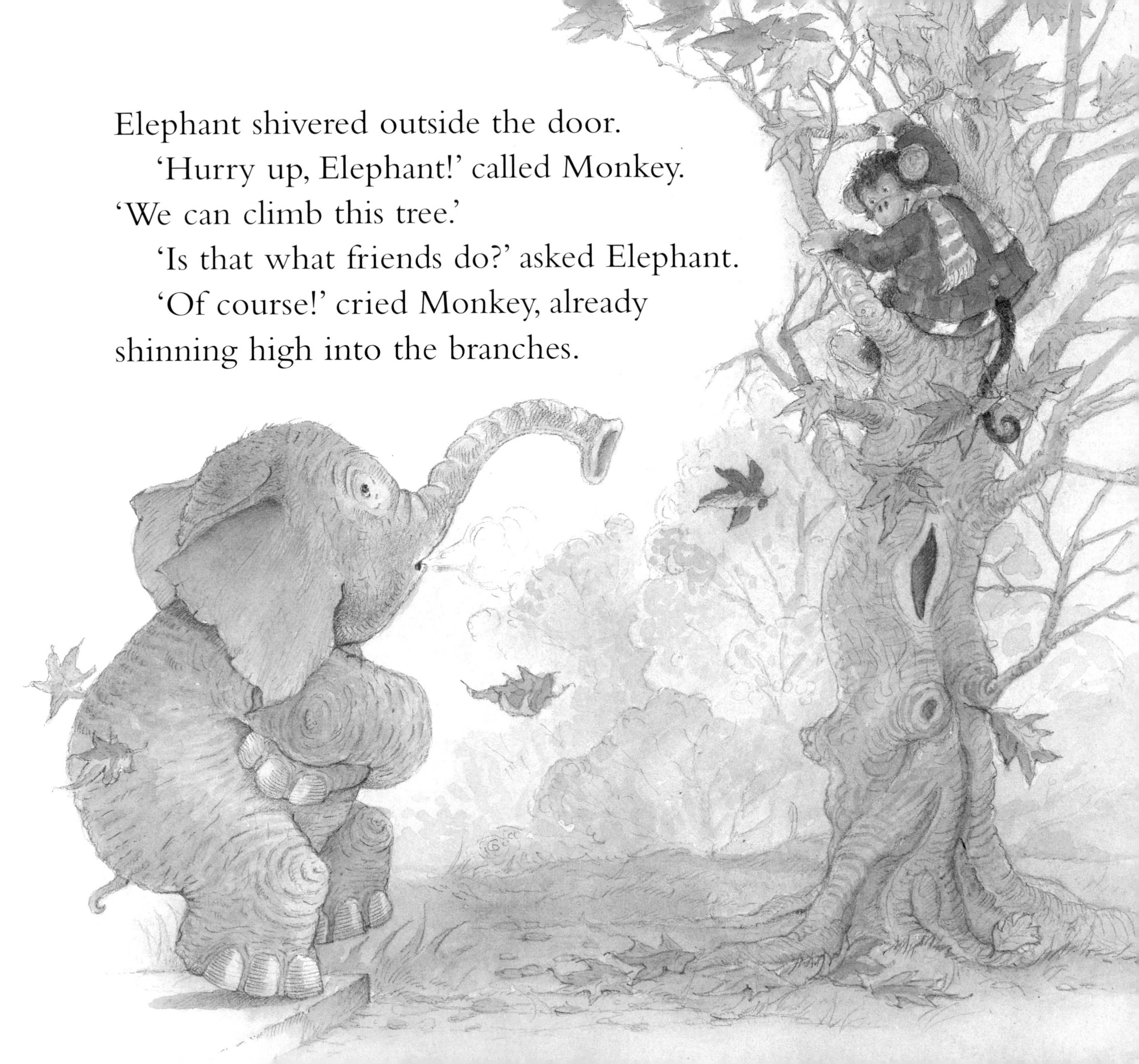

Elephant shivered outside the door.

'Hurry up, Elephant!' called Monkey. 'We can climb this tree.'

'Is that what friends do?' asked Elephant.

'Of course!' cried Monkey, already shinning high into the branches.

Elephant started to climb.
Crack went the branch.
Crash went Elephant.
‘**Ahhhhhhhhhhhhh!**’
cried Elephant.

‘Eee!’ cried Elephant.

‘Ow!’ cried Elephant.

‘I can’t climb.’

Monkey slid down the tree.

'Ah,' said Monkey.

'Eee,' said Monkey.

'Oh dear,' said Monkey, looking into a big hole, and not being able to see Elephant, *at all*.

Monkey was all alone.

Further along the bank Elephant sat gloomily. All alone.

Monkey came walking by.

'Oh, there you are, Elephant,' cried Monkey.

'Go away!' growled Elephant.

Monkey was very quiet. 'Elephant,' he said, 'you know I said I'd had lots of friends?'

'Yes,' sighed Elephant.

'Well,' said Monkey, 'none of them stayed friends for long.'

Elephant was quiet. Monkey was quiet. They were thinking.

'Elephant,' said Monkey, after a while, 'perhaps I got it all wrong.'

'Oh?' said Elephant.

'Elephant,' said Monkey. 'Perhaps friends are kind to each other and share things.'

'Oh!' said Elephant.

'Elephant,' said Monkey. 'Shall we try again?'
'Is that what friends do?' asked Elephant.

'Of course!' cried Monkey.
And they gave each other a great, big hug.